WE NEED TO TALK

THE TIME IS NOW

Sally-Anne Ward

BAD HAT PUBLISHING
Dedication

To those of you who have passed and to those of you who are survivors.

First published in Australia 2018 By Bad Hat Publishing.

2/ 30 The Avenue, Windsor Victoria, Australia.

E. david@badhatpublishing.com

w. badhatfilms.com.au/publishing

+61 (0) 451181713

Author: Sally-Anne Ward

Title: We Need to Talk

ISBN: 9780646985558 (paperback)

Subjects: Suicide

         Survival

         Bullying

A catalogue record for this book is available from the National Library of Australia

INTRODUCTION

Welcome to We Need To Talk - The Novel.

This is a young adult novel aimed at highlighting the need to talk and communicate effectively with each other to help raise awareness to youth bullying, mental health issues and suicide.

We follow the story of Bree, a teenager who appears to have it all together but is the victim of constant bullying that affects Bree so deeply with depression and anxiety that she tragically takes her own life.

We look at the aftermath of those she left behind and at where she sits in the spirit world now. It's not all doom and gloom in the novel as the Spirit Angel or God, as some people prefer, has a sense of humour about him.

If we can have an effect, open lines of communication or help one person connect in a much-needed way to save even just one life we will deem our mission a success.

Based on original screenplays written by David Raynor, who has also directed and produced a multi-international award winning short film of the same title, and original novel adapted by Sally-

Anne Ward. Both David and Sally-Anne have handled the topic with utmost respect and the delicacy such a topic deserves as they have thoroughly researched the issue and also have experience with loved ones who have fought, are fighting or have succumbed to mental illness.

trigger   warning

Parts of this novel are raw, real and may upset some readers, please, if this occurs, reach out for support, it is not our intention to cause upset, we just want to bridge the gap we have found to be missing.

Our motto in We Need To Talk is
that we need to love and take care
of   each other. Let's do that, share our
love and care with those around us.

CHAPTER ONE

SPIRIT ANGEL

Some days I sigh, for I'm not sure which is my preference, overseeing the universe or trying to make an art image out of fireworks, ice cream and flowers. Do you see my dilemma? Either option requires steadfast concentration and commitment. Art is relaxing, creativity is expressive, mind and soul food, regardless of the medium used to create. I am passionate about art and colour and creating, why do you think earth is such a visually beautiful place? I made it that way, but a lot of people nowadays don't 'see' it. Sighing again I return to keeping watch over the universe. There will be time for the other later. I get some time at the end of the days in earth time, The Lull I call it, where half the world is falling asleep and the other half is waking up. It's a quiet time where the universe doesn't require a constant eye.

Oh, I should probably introduce myself. I am Spirit Angel, some call me God, Allah, Buddha, Jehovah, Zeus, call me whatever you like. For I am whatever you conceive me to be, it really doesn't matter, we are all the same, energy filled beings, some in human form having an experience called *life*. I don't get around in a long white robe all the time either. Some days yes, I do wear a robe, some days a hula skirt, sometimes just a sarong!

But I am concerned dear humans, and if I'm completely honest I am becoming sadder with each orbit around your planet earth. Why am I sad? Well, I'm glad you asked. I'm sad because I am seeing souls lift from the earth daily, DAILY I say, and this worries me because it is becoming too common. I am seeing souls lift themselves from the earth. Young, beautiful, pure souls, souls of all shapes, ages and colours choosing to leave because they can't take it anymore. Catching the young souls is the most heartbreaking. Each tell me the same things as I embrace their brokenness, that they couldn't get anyone to listen to them, they weren't heard and eventually they gave up and left. My frustration, the frustration that hurts my heart is that try as I do, I couldn't stop them. I am juggling here. I have tried to get them to see their lives in their dreams, when I know they're hurting too much, how good their lives would be if they stayed, but they are too sad to see. I try too, to make the adults see and understand but they don't listen either, they're too busy, too caught up in their own heads. Hence the fireworks and things. Even if it does make a mess, it's fun and I think we would all agree that we need a lot more fun around the place.

Apologies for that slight digression (though once I do master the fireworks and ice cream flower arrangement image I will be sure to make a grand announcement about it). I see, with growing frustration, the widening gap in communication, the distance between humans, more connected than ever before thanks to the wonders of technology and social media. Yet even with those newfangled things people are becoming more isolated, disconnected, lonely, falling into depression. Talking has become a rare art and it needs to make a comeback, a strong one. Humans have forgotten how to love and take care of each other. They don't know how to connect or are perhaps scared to out of fear of being shut down, or ridiculed, or made to feel worse than they already do, and it's not okay, not at all. All living

3

souls need to talk, to connect, to really love and care for each other again, for the good of humanity.

I am trying desperately to turn earth around, to save it and all the sad souls on it. I am trying to shift the negative to positive, it is necessary. Later on, I will tell you about a particularly special planet, the heart of existence if you like, but not yet...

CHAPTER TWO

The melody of my phone alarm starts playing, bleary eyed I tap snooze and roll over onto my stomach. I don't want to wake up, don't want to get up. It's too hard and I'm too tired. I fall back asleep, the alarm sounds again, groaning I turn it off and lay staring at the ceiling. Why do I have to deal with yet another day? Why can't I wake up feeling good, just for once, wake up feeling happy, just for this week even. It seems so long since I've felt that way that I can't really remember how it *does* feel to wake up feeling good. It's my birthday in two days' time. I should be excited but I'm not, I'm full of dread, but that's also how I feel about life in general. I drag myself out of bed and get dressed. I survey myself in the mirror, I look as hellish as I feel. *Deep breaths Bree, deep breaths.* I watch myself breathe in the mirror, I can feel the anxiety building physically in my body and it makes me want to run. Instead I pick up my bag and head down to the kitchen. *Today,* I think to myself, *today is the day I will talk to Mum, tell her how I've been feeling, ask for her help.*

Planting a smile on my face I go into the kitchen. I know I'm running late but don't care and hope that Mum doesn't notice. She usually doesn't, she is usually too busy rushing around trying to get ready for work and organise Ben my younger brother.

'Morning Mum.' I force a smile as I pour a bowl of cereal and go to make coffee.

'Oh Bree, morning, sorry, I'm trying to remember where Ben left his runners.'

'At the front door.'

She looks at me. 'Really? How do you know? I swear he said he looked there.'

'I tripped over them last night when I got home.'

Mum kisses my cheek. 'You are seriously a godsend.' She rushes out of the kitchen, her heels clicking on the floor tiles, to round up Ben's shoes. I sit down to eat my cereal, it tastes like cardboard, why doesn't food seem to have flavour anymore? Maybe it's just me. I force myself to swallow each mouthful, it feels like stones going down my throat. Mum comes rushing back into the kitchen. I take a deep breath. *Breathe, speak, breathe.* I pep talk myself in my head. *She's my Mum, she will listen.*

'Mum, can we talk, just for a minute? Please?'

She is only half listening. Oh god, why did I choose now? I shouldn't have bothered. I should have waited, I don't know why I had to blurt that out right now. Idiot. I am an idiot.

'Sure, what about?' She is rustling around in her handbag.

'Nothing, it doesn't matter, it can wait.'

Mum looks at her phone, I watch her frown then look at her watch.

'Dammit. Bree is there any chance you can get Ben to school? My boss has called an early meeting, I have to leave now.'

'Yeah, sure.' I feel instantly weighted, I don't have the energy to say *no* and that *I just want to*

7

go back to bed. She unearths her car keys from inside her handbag.

'Bree, you really are my angel, thank you. We'll talk tonight okay? Can it wait until then?' She at least looks concerned. I nod and force a smile.

'I promise and thank you again darling.' She kisses me on the forehead, grabs her bag and phone, rushes off to find Ben. I sit at the table with my eyes closed and listen as she makes her way through the house, I take a deep breath when I hear the front door bang shut. I drag myself off the chair as Ben comes in.

'Hey sis, can we buy breakfast on the way to school?' He flutters his eyes at me and pretends to beg. I fall for it, I can't say no to him. He is one of the few things I have left that makes me *feel emotion.* I love this kid to bits.

'Didn't you have breakfast already?'

'Well, yes, but I'm still hungry.' He looks sheepish and then starts laughing.

'You're always hungry.' I'm genuinely smiling and it feels good. Ben stands up tall and puffs out his chest.

'I'm a growing boy sis.' I giggle a real giggle for the first time in two days.

'Come on then, get your bag and let's go.'

'Yes!' He fist pumps the air and races off, I get my bag and keys. Ben runs in front of me.

'Race you outside sis!' He wins but I don't care, he wins too because of how good he's made me feel but I don't tell him that. I look up and notice that it's sunny, how many sunny days haven't I noticed? This bothers me. I love the sun, love the feeling of it on my skin, I make a mental note to promise to look up every day.

CHAPTER 3

We ride our bikes, Ben follows me, on a whim I take us to Maccas.

Ben rides up beside me.

'Uh, sis, this isn't the school.' I look at him over my shoulder.

'Yeah, I know. So? I decided we are going to eat in.'

'But I'll be late for school.'

'So? I'll sign you in late, I just want to hang with you for a while.'

'Yes! Best morning ever!' We lean our bikes against a wall out of everyone else's way and go inside. I love this kid so much, he's one of the few things left that makes me happy. *Please let it be enough to make me stay.*

I grab a table while Ben waits for our order, I watch him waiting and I can't believe how quickly he is growing up. I feel my heart swell and my eyes fill, I really hope my love for him will be enough to keep me here.

I didn't realise I had become lost in my thoughts until Ben almost drops the tray as he clambers back to the table.

'Are you okay sis?'

'Yep, why's that?' I plaster a smile on my face.

'You just looked really sad for a minute.' I feel the weight descend again.

'I don't know, I do feel sad, I just don't know why, every day it's different.' Ben looks really worried now. He comes and sits next to me and puts his arm around me and plants a kiss on my cheek.

'I love you big sis.' He gives me a squeezy hug.

'I love you too little brother.' *Please, please let him be enough to keep me here.* We eat our breakfast talking and laughing and then Ben looks at his watch.

'Shit Bree, we are really late!' he smirks at me.

'Hey, no swearing or I'll tell Mum.' Ben starts laughing.

'No you won't because then I'll tell her you made me late for school.' I start laughing again, it feels so good. I hope this mood holds on for the whole day.

'Alright then smartass, we are even. Let's get moving.'

We arrive at Ben's school still mucking around and giggling. I sign him in at the office then take him to his classroom even though he can do it himself. I just wanted to have a few more minutes with him, wasn't ready to leave him just yet. Grabbing him in a hug I ruffle his hair and kiss his forehead.

'See you tonight little brother, have a good day.'

'I will.' He smiles and opens his classroom door. I turn and head back down the corridor. I hear footsteps behind me, it's Ben.

'Thanks for this morning sis, you rock, I love you. I hope you have a happy day.' He runs back to his classroom.

'I love you too.' I call out to his retreating back.

The further away I walk from him, the more I feel like I've left my heart with him. The thought of the rest of the day feels endless. I am anxious now about talking to Mum tonight, I kinda wish I hadn't said anything now. Maybe she will have forgotten it, so I decide not to mention anything and hope she really has forgotten or has her mind full of her job like usual. If I were braver I would tell her that since she started this job a year ago she seems to have distanced from me. It hurts because we used to be so close, now I just feel like her slave, *Bree can you do this*, *Bree can you please do that*. In all honesty I don't mind because at least she still notices me, I just feel like she doesn't *see* me anymore. Maybe if she stopped and really looked at me she might notice that I'm not okay, that I'm fragile and don't know what to do. But I guess we all walk past people every day and unless we had little thought bubbles above our heads we don't ever really know what anyone is thinking. Maybe some of the smartest people are saddest, maybe some homeless people are happiest, who can tell unless we ask? Plus, everyone is always so *'busy'* with life doing what they do, would they even care if they did notice or ask?

CHAPTER 4

SPIRIT ANGEL

Oh dear. This is precisely what I'm talking about. Bree. She needs to talk, yet is afraid to, this is not good. I am going to keep an eye on her, she is a special soul, oh who am I kidding? Every soul is special. Some shine brighter and some don't shine so much, but all souls are necessary, every soul has a valid reason for being alive, to touch the lives of each other. I feel Bree's pain and I am desperately trying to shift her thinking, take the heaviness off her heart and mind. I am fearful for her because she has fallen so quickly. I wish there was more of me to go around, to help me with the juggling. I pray she will talk. I pray her mother will listen, that someone will listen. Earth needs her, she is 'aware', she is a thinker, she has worked out the need for communication. I pray she stays, I will work hard to make her try. Bree! I want to yell, talk! Yell! Scream! Please make yourself be heard! You are necessary! I need you to know that nothing
would, or will be the same if you didn't or don't exist! Please hold on!

CHAPTER 5

I put my bike in the student bike park at my school, and just stand in silence staring. I feel my breathing quicken, my hands are clammy, tingling and shaking, my heart starts pounding and I feel dizzy. My mouth goes dry and I can't swallow, I break out in a sweat, anxiety rages through my body. I want to fight this feeling but I'm too tired. I want to run as far away as I can go but also want to be so still and unmoving. It's a weird and awful feeling. I slump down on a bench seat and close my eyes and wait for the peak of it to pass. It tires me out more, I just want to go home and go back to bed.

I feel like the world can see what's going on inside me and I hate it. I hate feeling this way, I don't want to feel this way anymore but I don't know what to do. I hope Mum can help, there's no point in asking Dad since he cleared out and got himself a new family. The surge of anger that this thought gives me gets me moving, albeit with leaden steps toward the building here today, I promised my friends I would be here so we can finalise our plans for tomorrow. *Plans, yay right, why can't I be happy about having 'plans', anyone else would be.* But to me it just feels like an obligation. I even feel guilty about thinking that way because these plans are for me. I should be happy about it and I am, I just wish I could *feel* it properly.

Entering the building I feel the anxiety trying to start again, I try to ignore it and concentrate on each step I take. I stop half way up the hall, sigh, and decide to go to the cafeteria for a hot chocolate, then give myself five minutes of doing nothing to pull myself together. I like this feeling, the being decisive in my actions and knowing that it's okay to just stop for five minutes and do nothing but sit and breathe. I take my drink and go and sit at a table near the window so I can watch the world go by while I concentrate on pulling myself together. Fortunately, it's during class time, so I am alone aside from the cafeteria staff.

I'm lost in my thoughts thinking about how happy I was last year; how so damn happy I was. I think I laughed more last year than I had in my whole life, it was an awesome time. Myself and my best friend since the start of high school, Danielle, decided way back then that when we made it to year 11 we would take a holiday, and we did. We both got part time jobs and saved as much as we could to do it and we did. It's something I am so proud of and so glad we did this. We made memories that will last as long as we live, however long that will be.

At the moment, it's Danielle and Ben that are the only reasons I'm still here. My Mum and I used to be so close but everything changed when her and Dad split up. I had just come back from being away with Danielle, high on the thrill of having been to so many places and seen so much, and then I come home to Mum having to get a fulltime job just to afford to live, and we have drifted apart. She's always busy now. Like I get that she needs to do it, but I just miss how we used to be, and feel alone. Thank god for Ben and Danielle.

It was after coming back from overseas that I started to go downhill, maybe I used up all my happiness in other countries. Can that happen? Or is it just silly to think that way? But that's how it feels. Like maybe I crammed my whole lifetime of happiness into a holiday. Had I been happy before that?

I think hard. Yes, when I was little I was happy, and at primary school. I see now the turning point was secondary school, that's when the bullying started. I was so excited to start secondary school, so thrilled to have clicked with Danielle straight away and become best friends. I thought becoming and being a teenager were going to be the best years of my life but I was wrong, maybe my expectation was too high? I don't know, I don't think so. I mean we all start there not really having any idea of what we are doing and just go along with life, yeah. I never expected it to be perfect every day but I never expected it to be so awful at times either. I thought that when I finished high school the bullying would stop but it didn't. I didn't bank on still copping hell via social media. I just can't understand what they are hoping to achieve. Like, does it make them feel good doing it? Do they get some kind of stupid thrill out of it? Don't they have a conscience? Has it ever occurred to them to think about how they would feel if people did it to them? It's pointless and nasty. I was so lost in my thoughts I didn't hear anyone approaching me until a bag is dumped on the table in front of me. I look up as Tako, my male best friend, flops himself into the chair opposite me.

'Hey, you okay?' I snap out of my thoughts.

'Yeah, why?'

'It's not like you to skip a class, I kept waiting for you to arrive.'

'Sorry, I had to take Ben to school for Mum and was late so skipped class.'

'Ah. Okay. I sent you some texts and got worried when you didn't reply. I was worried.'

'Oh, I haven't even looked at my phone.'

Tako purses his lips and looks at me. 'Since when?'

'Since when what?' I'm confused by why he asked me that.

'That you looked at your phone.'

'I don't know, two hours. Why?' I feel dread setting in.

'Um… one of the bitch brigade posted a screenshot on Facebook and Instagram of you, someone edited a Wikipedia page… they posted a school photo of you under *slut*.'

I snatch my phone out of my bag and go to the page and sure enough there it is. Tako is staring at me, my body feels like it is turning to liquid and I start to shake.

Tako reaches across and takes my phone out of my hand. I stare at him. 'I'm so sorry Bree, I've reported it and checked the page and it's been taken down everywhere.'

I can feel the tears falling out of my eyes even though I didn't feel them start.

'Baby please don't cry, they're not worth it.'

My whole body is trembling and I cling to

Tako's hand. 'Why won't they quit?'

'Please try not to let them get to you, rise above it, please Bree, they're not worth it.

'That's easy for you to say, it's not you, this hurts Tako and I've had enough.' I stand up and pick up my bag, 'I'm going home.'

'I'm coming too.' Tako stands up as well and takes my hand.

'No, you stay, you can't skip classes.'

'I care more about you so I'm coming too.' I feel torn between relief and wanting to be alone.

'So, that's settled then, then I'm taking you out for the day.'

I sigh, I don't have the strength to resist.

'Okay.'

I start walking on auto pilot outside. Tako kind of bounces as he walks, he's like a half-excited puppy all the time. It normally makes me smile but today I just notice it but don't smile.

'I'll grab my crap and meet you at your place in fifteen minutes.' I nod and keep walking. Tako takes his phone out of his pocket and I see him make a call.

I arrive home and see Danielle sitting on my doorstep. What is she doing here? I drag myself off my bike and walk toward her, she comes to meet me and grabs me in a hug.

'What are you doing here?'

She grins at me, I can feel her happy energy oozing from her. How I wish I could feel that way all the time again.

'Wagging, like you.'

'I'm not wagging, I just… couldn't…' I feel my facial expression change. *Hold it together Bree* I think to myself.

'Hey, Bree, it's me, let it out.' Danielle puts her hands on my shoulders and stares into my eyes, I stare back.

'I can't… it's stuck.' She hugs me and I still can't cry.

CHAPTER 6

Tako and Danielle make me wear a blindfold and put me in the backseat of Tako's car. Tako is the only one of us that has a car and license, he started school a year later than the rest of us and then had to repeat a year in primary school; it used to bother him but he sees now that it has given him wisdom and he is grateful for that, I am too.

'Where are you guys taking me?'

'On an adventure.' I can hear the smile in Tako's voice.

'Danielle, you saw what was posted didn't you?' She is quiet for a moment before she answers me.

'Yeah, I did, I didn't respond to them. They're not worth it.' She goes quiet again. That makes me nervous because I know Danielle so well.

'What did you do then?'

'Screenshotted their bullshit and sent it to their parents and told them it was high time their immature asshole kids grew the fuck up. Sent it by messenger too so I can see they've read it.'

'Oh shit. Danielle...' I hear her turn around from the front seat.

'No, not *oh shit*, they need to be aware of what their kids are doing, they need to know it hasn't stopped. Enough is enough, and I'm sorry, I know we say rise above it and ignore it and shit like that but I know it still gets you down, so does Tako. We would and will walk through fire for you. I personally think it's because you are everything. You're smart, kind, there's a quality to you that not many people possess, and that's why I think you are their target. They wish they had those qualities, and in my opinion, they stupidly think that if they can break that in you then they can have it for themselves. It's an idiotic way to think.'

'Danielle, everyone has qualities about them that makes them targets for different things.

Some people get picked on for being fat, nerdy, because they've got red hair and freckles, things like that.' I sigh.

'Yes, I know, but those things I pointed out are why you are their target and it's not okay, there is no reason that's okay for anyone to be mean just for the sake of being mean.'

I hear her turn around and she puts some music on. I settle into the seat and let the music into my mind. Danielle has great taste in music, she just knows what's needed and when.

I must have drifted off to sleep because the next thing I knew I opened my eyes to Danielle's face grinning into mine, she must have taken the blindfold off.

'Hey sleepyhead, wake up, we are here'

'Where?'

'Early birthday present. Come on.' She drags me out of the car and I smell the sea air and feel the sunshine on my face.

They've brought me to a beach, my favourite place to ever be is on a beach, I don't care where, it soothes me and makes me happy. I feel a rush of energy and what I can only describe as pure joy. I hadn't noticed Tako lagging behind us, I was just drawn to the sand and water. I kick off my shoes and bury my feet in the sun-warmed sand. I then realise I haven't got a towel or swimwear.

'Guys, I haven't got a towel or...'

Danielle doesn't let me finish my sentence.

'Surprise!' She's still grinning and Tako raises two bags he had hidden behind his back and passes them to me. Looking inside I see exactly what I need.

I grab both of them in a hug. 'I love you two, I really do.'

'We love you too.' Danielle squeezes a bit harder.

'Happy early birthday!' Tako plants a kiss on my cheek.

I pull out the towel and swimwear from one bag and they're perfect. I look in the other bag and it's got all my favourite snacks, as well as an inflatable palm tree, inflatable ball, a hair tie with a hibiscus on it and a plastic pineapple shaped cup. I burst out laughing. 'Did you two pre-plan this?' They look at each other, then back at me.

'Kinda, when I left you at school I called Danielle and told her I was worried and didn't know what to do...' Danielle cuts him off.
'And I was like "let's start her birthday early." Plus, we are a bit selfish and wanted to have some special birthday time with just you.' Danielle points back towards the car park. 'Go get changed.'

I salute her and turn and wander off to get changed, still feeling the energy of happiness,

29

taking deep long breaths of the sea air. I cannot wait to dive into the water. *Please let it be as perfect as I need it to be, I need this feeling, I need to hold this feeling, this mood, this happiness instead of anxiety. Please, please, please.* I finish changing and pull my hair into the hibiscus hair tie then rush back to Danielle and Tako.

Danielle is blowing up the ball, Tako the palm tree, he looks funny with a plastic palm tree protruding from his face and I burst out laughing. Danielle finishes blowing up the ball and hits it towards Tako, he responds by whacking the ball with the palm tree. Danielle pulls out her phone and gets some reggae music going, she softly takes my hand and looks into my eyes.

'Jamaica, remember Jamaica.' My eyes instantly fill but I smile as well. I nod. I absolutely loved Jamaica, when we went there it was my favourite place, I never wanted to leave. It's my literal *happy place*.

We spend the day swimming, laughing, eating and mucking around, listening to reggae, dancing in the sand and sunbaking. All thoughts of my dark morning and the social media crap forgotten and out of my mind. Eventually I think to look at my phone, I text Mum and Ben, it's late in the day and check in. They're home and good, so we decide to have fish and chips for dinner and watch the sunset.

Still feeling happy when they dropped me home, I jogged inside and was met by Ben watching TV and Mum in the kitchen stacking the dishwasher.

'Hi, I'm home.' I startled her and she drops a plate which smashed into tiny pieces on the floor.

'Oh woops, hi Bree, how are you darling? Ben!' she called out 'Can you please bring me the broom and dustpan from the laundry?' 'Yep.' I hear Ben move.

'Here, let me help.' I say, wanting to help but also hoping to connect with her. We start gently picking the pieces up, Mum sighs.

'This is the icing on the cake for today.' She sighs again.

'Have you had a bad day?' She looks at me and our eyes connect. *Yes, she sees me, yes.* Mum goes to say something else as Ben comes around the corner of the kitchen riding the broom like it's a horse and swinging the dustpan. He makes us both laugh.

'Out of the way ladies, Cowboy Ben is here to save the day.' He shoos us out of the kitchen by pretending to sweep us, so Mum and I go into the lounge room. I desperately want to bring that brief connection back.

'Mum, can I get you a wine?'

'Oh, yes please darling, that would be great.' I quickly go and get a glass of wine, pass it to her then sit on the other end of the couch to her. She smiles at me, I feel my hopes rise and my courage to talk rises too.

'Mum, I'm having a really hard time lately...' I start.

'Oh, me too honey, it's exhausting, isn't it? Sorry if I've been distracted but it's just so hard trying to do everything, work, run this house, make sure you and Ben are okay, keep up with the yard and bills, everything.' She stares off into nothing.

'I understand most of that but I guess I just feel like we've lost our connection, we hardly talk anymore and I miss it.' I feel my heartbeat accelerate and anxiety creep in.

'Bree, of course we talk, I make sure I see you and Ben every day and we have dinner at the table every night like we always have.'

'I know, but I mean *really* talk, I'm struggling with stuff lately and I want to talk to you about it, just you, like we used to.' Now my hands are clammy. 'I feel like we've lost our closeness that we had.'

'I'm sorry you feel that way but I've had a lot on my mind too, since your father left...' At that moment Ben comes around the corner with the dustpan full of plate shards.

'Mum, where do you want this?'

'In the outside bin thanks Ben.'

'Do I have to? It's dark outside.' Mum gets up off the couch.

'I'll do it then.' She takes the dustpan from Ben, he drops onto the couch next to me.

'So, did you have a good day sis?' I feel my heart warm so I tell him about my day. I take the now deflated palm tree out of my bag and give it to him, he inflates it and cracks up laughing.

'Can I have it?' He asks.

'No, it was an early birthday present.'

'Oh please?'

'No.' I'm trying to keep a straight face.

'Can we share it?' He gives me his best puppy dog eyes.

'Okay then, it's ours.' He launches off the couch with it.

'Awesome! Thanks sis! I'm going to take some selfies with it and make a cool profile pic.' I can't help but laugh.

Mum comes back in, picks up her wine glass then goes into the kitchen. I decide to follow her.

She has tipped the wine out and is now taking headache tablets with water.

'Are you okay?' I ask.

'Yeah, fine, just a headache, probably stress from work. Or your father. Who knows these days.' She pauses then comes to me and hugs me. 'I'm sorry Bree, you don't need to hear that. So, what was it you wanted to talk about? Your birthday? Have you decided whether you want to go out or me cook a roast? Are you inviting anyone?'

'No Mum, I wanted to talk about how I've been feeling lately, it hasn't been good.' I notice her take a side glance at the clock on the wall, it's 9.15pm.

'Do you want me to make you a doctor's appointment for a check-up?' She at least has the decency to look concerned.

'No, Mum, not as in that way, as in my head not feeling good.' Just then her phone rings, she answers it.

'Hang on, I'll be one sec. *Hello Gloria speaking.*' She touches me lightly on the arm, though it feels like a burn. She answers her phone, it's work. I watch her talking and opening her laptop and listen to some work talk about a missing document that should have been emailed or *blah blah*. She has completely forgotten I'm there.

'As crap as I am feeling, I had a great day today, thanks for asking,' I whisper quietly to myself as I go to my bedroom. I shower and get into bed. Laying there staring at the ceiling I decide to call Dad. I listen to his phone ring, he finally answers. 'Hey Dad.'

'Hey princess, how are you?' he sounds distracted.

'Are you busy? Can we talk?' I hear him hesitate before answering.

'Yeah, sure. What's up?'

'I don't feel okay.' I hear the shudder in my voice and kick myself for it.

'What do you mean? Are you sick?' I hear him cover the phone and I hear him say something muffled to someone. Great, he hasn't got time to talk to his own daughter, clearly his 'new' family now take priority.

'No, but I think I need help and I don't know what to do.'

'Oh, have you talked to your mum?'

'I tried, like I'm trying to talk to you now.' He must have heard a tone in my voice because his changed.

'Bree, I'm sorry, can I call you tomorrow, it's just we've got visitors that are about to leave.'

'Okay, don't worry about it. I'll work it out.'

'Thanks princess, I am sorry, I promise I'll call you in the morning when I'm on my way to work.'

'Yeah okay.'

'Thanks, love you Bree.'

'Yeah, love you too.' I stab the end button on my phone. The feeling of anxiety is rising, and a desperation, I need it to stop. I decide to call Aunt Helen, she answers on the second ring.

'Hey baby girl? How's my favourite niece? Not long now until your birthday! What are we doing for it? I can't wait! I'm so excited! I can still remember changing your nappies when you were a baby! I can't wait to give you your present, I've worked really hard on it and I think you'll love it!' The way she answered, sounding so pleased to hear from me brings a lump to my throat and I can't speak for a minute. 'Bree? Are you there? Or did you bum dial me?' A weird sounding giggle comes out of me.

'Bree, are you okay?' I hear her voice shift from excitement to concern and it brings the lump back to my throat. 'Right, I feel like you're not okay so I will stay on the line until you feel like you can talk. I don't care if I stay here listening to silence, when you're ready or feel like it, then talk. I make another sound. 'Bree honey, has something happened?' That's all I needed to hear, it opens a gate.

'Aunt Helen I don't feel good, I'm so unhappy, everything is wrong, I feel invisible, the bullying is still going, I hate it. Dad's got his new family and Mum's too busy and I hate waking up in the mornings. I don't want to get up, I don't want to function, I hate my life, I hate life. I want out Aunt Helen, I want out, but I don't want to leave Ben or you or Danielle, but I want all the pain to stop. I can't handle it, I can't breathe anymore, I don't want to breathe anymore, I don't want my birthday, I want to disappear...'

'Bree, breathe, slow down, breathe.' Her voice has taken on a serious tone, now I feel bad that I've freaked her out.

'Aunty Helen I'm so sorry, I shouldn't have bothered you.

'Darling you are never a bother, I'm just pissed off that I'm in the next state, I'm currently searching for the next flight out so I can get to you.' This breaks me, that she would drop everything to help me.

'It's okay, I'll be okay.'

'You don't sound okay. Have you spoken to your Mum? Or that dickhead that is meant to be your dad?' The way she says it makes me giggle.

'I tried. Mum's too busy with work, Dad's too distracted by his new family and I don't want to burden Ben because he's so young. I didn't know what to do so I called you. I hope that was okay.'

'Of course, it's okay, I couldn't care less if it was 3am I would always answer the phone for you. Do you feel like you need help right now?'

'No, I feel better just talking to you.'

'Have you been thinking about ending it? Suicidal?' I pause before answering, I don't know whether to be completely honest because I don't want to scare her.

'Sometimes yes, but not at the moment. I feel like I desperately need help but don't know what to do.'

'It's okay, if anyone understands I do, I swear I will help you and get whatever help you need to be okay.'

'I know, that's why I called you, you *get* me like nobody else does.'

'I'm going to keep talking to you until you fall asleep and then in the morning when you wake up I will still be here waiting to hear you, okay?' I feel my heart swell with love.

'Okay.'

'Unless I can get a flight, then I'll have to hang up but that will be the only reason this call will end, and if that happens then I want you to call me as soon as you wake up. Promise?'

'I promise.'

'Man, the internet here is shit, I wish I knew who the boss of internet connections was so I could go snot him.' I laugh out loud. 'So, tell me about your day and what's been happening, then I'll bore you shitless with the crap I've been doing.' I start with bad stuff like the bullying and latest social media stuff, then tell her about making Ben late for school, then my day at the beach. She says all positive things. Aunt Helen has had a tough life but always finds silver linings and it reminds me that things can be bad but then good comes along again. I need to remember and hold on to that. I eventually fall asleep and she keeps her word. When I wake up she is still there, sounding tired, but there.

'Morning Aunt Helen.' I mumble.

'Morning beautiful girl, are you okay?' I do a mental check list.

'Yes, actually yes, I think I am okay.'

'Good, now go shower and start your day, call me anytime, I've changed my flight and I'll be back tonight instead of tomorrow morning.'

'You didn't have to do that.' I feel humbled.

'I know I didn't, I wanted to. I've been in your shoes Bree, I won't let you down, I promised you that when you were a baby and I won't break a promise.' I hear the love in her voice and it reaches *me*.

'I love you Aunt Helen.'

'I love you too baby girl.'

'Bree, keep this thought in your head all day, do it for me, make it your mantra, remember this – *Nothing would be the same if you didn't exist.* Yes, it sounds deep and heavy but it's true, occupy your mind with thinking about the profoundness of it, the depth of it and then look at the big picture of it.'

'Thank you, Aunt Helen, I like it, I promise I will keep it in my mind.'

I hang up and again drag myself out of bed to start the day feeling like I've finally got a lifeline. *Maybe, maybe I can hold on, please let me hold on. Nothing would be the same if I didn't exist.*

I put some music on while I shower and get ready for the shopping trip I've got planned with Danielle, Tako, Billie, Sophie and Scarlet. I'm anxious but keen to spend time with them all. I can never shop in malls alone, too much noise, lights and people, but I can do it with my friends and we always have fun. Once ready, I wander into the kitchen for breakfast. Ben is doing his homework at the last minute like usual.

'Hey little bro, can you actually taste what you're eating or are you just hungry?' I ask him with a smile. He gives me a mouth full of cereal with a lopsided grin.

'I'm multi-tasking sis.'

'I see. You're doing great at it too. Are you saving that glob of cereal on your top as a snack for school?' He looks down at his top.

'Oh man! How did I miss my mouth?'

'You must have been too focused on your homework dear brother.' He looks at me sheepishly.

'Well, yeah, maybe, I kinda wanted Nicole to notice me 'cos she's really nice and so pretty and...' 'And you want to impress her.' I add. 'Yeah...' he blushes a bright red, 'she's so smart and I think she likes me and I don't want her to think I'm dumb.'

'You are far from dumb, and anyway, she should like you for who you are not for how smart you are.' He stands up and looks at me.

'I'm going to go change my top, which is annoying because I really like this one and I hoped Nicole might too.' He starts to leave the room and then hesitates, he grabs me in one of his all-consuming bear hugs. 'I wish I was as smart as you too. Nicole reminds me of you in ways, so calm and nice. I wish everyone was like you sis.' With that he races off to change as Mum comes in the kitchen.

'Morning love, how are you?' she asks while her facial expression still looks bewildered by Ben's haste. Ben never rushes.

'I'm good.'

'What's with your brother?'

'Oh, I pointed out that he had cereal slopped on his top so he's changing it.' She raises her eyebrows at this.

'Serious? He never cares what he looks like, I'm flat out getting him to brush his hair.' We both laugh.

'He likes a girl.' I say.

'Ah... well then, wow, yeah I guess he is at that age.'

'Yes, he is.' We share a knowing look. 'Can I make you a coffee Mum? I'm having one.' She looks at her watch.

'Actually, yes, let's have it outside together.' This makes my heart sing. 'I'll grab my shoes and bag and be right out.' She almost crashes into Ben who has come rushing back into the kitchen.

'Gotta go guys.' he says.

'What's the hurry? Mum asks.

'No reason, just don't want to be late.' He slinks towards the door.

'A girl perhaps?' Mum asks. Ben blushes all over again.

'Maybe... aw man, can't a boy have a secret in this house?'

'*Ooo,* so it is a girl.' Mum follows Ben around the kitchen as he gathers his school stuff.

'Yes Mum, ask Bree, she will tell you 'cos I just told her.' She grabs his face and kisses his cheek.

'Go, have a good day, see you tonight.'

'Bye Mum.' He races off and in his usual style comes back and plants a kiss on both mine and Mum's faces. 'Bye sis.' Then just before he shuts the front door behind him he calls out 'But you two will always be my favourite ladies first.' We both laugh and share another look, my heart soars again, we have connected. I hand Mum her coffee and we go and sit out the back. Mum takes a sip and closes her eyes for a second, savouring it. I savour the moment.

'You really do make the best coffee Bree.'

'Thanks, it's liquid life isn't it.' she laughs.

'Yes, it is! So, are you okay? Do you want to talk? I'm so sorry about last night. I wanted to say

47

you looked so radiant when you got home, like when you came home from your holiday.'

'I didn't think you noticed.'

'I did, I just stupidly didn't think to say so until later. My brain is overloaded lately.'

'It's okay.'

'No Bree, it's not, I feel awful about it. So, can I make you a doctor's appointment? Do you want me to come with you? I can make time early next week.' She frowns and I watch her face, I feel like an inconvenience.

'No, it's okay, I'll do it.'

'Are you sure?'

'Yes, I'm okay today.' I hesitate, 'It's you I want to talk to though, not a doctor.' She looks at me oddly. 'I miss you Mum, I miss us, we don't connect much anymore and it hurts.' She looks stunned.

'Oh, Bree I'm sorry, I thought we were okay, I'm trying to juggle so much...'

'I know Mum, I get it, but it's hard. It's been hard for me lately.' I start feeling relief as she is listening to me, actually listening, and it feels good.

'You've never said, I wish you'd said something before now.'

'I tried Mum, you're always distracted and I understand that, but I still need you.'

'Oh sweetheart...' She stands and draws me into a hug, I can smell her perfume and lotions, she smells like Mum. I close my eyes and commit those scents and the feeling of her hug to memory. Just then her phone rings and the moment is gone, she shuts down and slips straight into business mode, I can tell it's a work call. I grab my keys and bag, kiss her on the cheek as she is putting papers in her laptop bag with her phone tucked under her ear, smile and wave, then leave.

CHAPTER 7

SPIRIT ANGEL

Oh thank goodness, Bree opened up to her Aunty, I can't tell you the relief I feel about that. Her Aunt Helen is what I call an 'earth angel', an anchor between here and earth, as essential as every other human but they carry an energy in them that's different to other humans. I'm holding hope for Bree, sending her hope, praying she feels it and holds on. And she has tried, tried to connect with her mum. I hope they 'get there', hope that fresh line of communication stays open, but I fear for it, life is too busy. Remember world globes? They spun on a stand and collected dust, every home used to have them before technology was invented. Maybe some people still have them, maybe they've all turned to dust or hiding long forgotten in garages. Anyway, you know what I mean, that's kinda like what my job is. I sit here with this big world globe in front of me and I spin it and see what's happening *where*, and who needs *what* and *when*, and how quickly they need it.

I have to say it's getting harder to keep up, I wish I could be everywhere. It gets harder every day to keep up. Some souls fall so quickly that I couldn't help them, couldn't show or guide them, it frustrates me. And you know that thing called the solar system? That's kinda where I live. I can be anywhere, but generally I float around amongst the stars, sounds like magic doesn't it? It is in a lot of ways a beautiful view I must say, but also hard work, because while I'm watching earth I am also keeping an eye on a special planet, *Rosetta Duopolous*, the literal energy planet of life.

Rosetta Duopolous never used to need so much attention. It needs to be green to sustain life everywhere, yeah, every now and then there used to be parts that would turn red, when a war was going on or unrest somewhere. It requires positivity from emanated human energy to sustain it. It now needs a constant eye, as the balance of positive coming from humans has swung around to negative so fast, and it's not good. The negative energy it's absorbing instead, is sending it red, it's heating up and it concerns me. It concerns me greatly.

CHAPTER 8

I end up running five minutes late to meet my friends, they are waiting for me at the mall entrance. Billie comes rushing up to me and puts her hands on my shoulders like she hasn't seen me for weeks, yet it's been less than a week.

'Guess what Bree! I did it! Man, it feels good! Such a friggin' relief! And it was okay! It's all okay!' She nearly knocks me over in her enthusiasm.

'Did what? Billie, you've got so much going on it could be anything.' I laugh, her excitement is infectious and I'm grateful for it.

'I came out! To Mum and Dad! Actually, the whole family, at the dinner table, probably not the best place but I figured hey, everyone's together so why not? So, they all knew at once.' She's grinning widely.

'Wow! I'm stunned! Go you! What made you tell them at that moment?' She starts laughing.

'Well, they were all starting to bicker, you know, as families do when you stuff them all in one place together. I get sick of it you know, like every time we all get together there's some kind of disagreement. Anyway, they were banging on about bloody politics of all things and I was like *oh booooooooring!* And like ten minutes later they were still going and I was over it, so I said, "can someone please pass the salt and by the way I'm gay." Silenced them! It was classic!' Her smile is radiant.

'And they're cool with it?' I ask.

'Yes, Mum said later that she had thought maybe I was but wasn't sure how to talk to me about it and Dad's still in shock but just wants me to be happy.'

'How do *you* feel?

'Lighter to be honest. I feel like a cloud has been lifted, and in a few weeks I want to start and try to come off the anti-depressants. Mum thinks that by keeping my feelings about being gay, to myself, may have been the cause of my anxiety and depression and I think she's right.'

'That's so good, just take baby steps okay.'

'I will.' She hugs me tightly. 'Thank you for always being so supportive of me and for being such an awesome friend.'

'Aww! Thanks, but you don't need to thank me, I love you just the way you are.'

'I know, and that's one of the reasons I love you too.'

Tako and Danielle rush to me, they each take a side of me, Danielle links her arm through mine.

'Bree, please don't listen to anything that's about to come out of Tako's mouth. He thinks purple and white look nice together and I don't, I think purple and black look better together.' I look at Tako who is now rolling his eyes.

'No, well, yes, but... like for a guy!'

'What for a guy? Purple and black or purple and white?' I ask him.

'I don't know now, I've confused myself! I'm just trying to think of a new colour for my wardrobe...'

Danielle chimes in. 'What, aside from black? Or black tops with print on them, or black jeans with black shoes...'

Sophie and Scarlet arrive together and wave as they approach.

Tako seizes the moment to act the fool. 'Ladies! Save me! Danielle has no style!' He dramatically lands on his knees in front of them.

'Don't listen to him!' Danielle runs up to them as well, Billie and I hang back and watch.

'Style? Danielle has awesome style Tako.' Scarlet looks at Tako.

'Well, yes, but no, but...' Tako starts.

'Tako, your style is black, always has been, kinda like me.' Sophie does a twirl, we all laugh, she is wearing almost all black. Danielle smacks her own forehead and elbows Tako. Billie looks at me smirking.

'Children! That's enough sand pit squabbling, let's go shopping!' Billie claps her hands together

to round them up and we enter the mall, all happy,
all laughing.

CHAPTER 9

THE END

BREE

It's my birthday today. Happy birthday to me. 18. I am 18. I've woken up. I've made it this far. I can't go any further, I wanted to, I really did. I woke up this morning, I actually felt a bit of motivation, a small amount of excitement at it being my birthday but now I don't want to move. I'm laying rigid in my bed, staring blankly at the ceiling. Again. A repeat of many mornings, many mornings where I have felt this way and yet managed to continue.

The weight is too heavy today. I can't do this anymore, I can't do another eighteen years of this, eighteen weeks, eighteen days, eighteen hours, it's too heavy. My body feels like lead. Maybe this is how it feels to be dead. Still and unmoving, is there a peace to it? Or just the finality? The motivation I felt when I woke up is gone, the small ripple of excitement I felt about my birthday has gone. I woke up to my phone tinging and vibrating with messages on various platforms. They started out nice and full of love, from Aunt Helen, Ben has already done an Instagram post, Danielle, Tako and a few others have done Facebook statuses tagging me in a birthday post. All made me smile briefly. Briefly. Then I made a mistake. I read some comments, then I scrolled and found more posts and they were nasty. Really nasty. Too nasty. They're never going to quit, they've never lost interest or found another target, this is never going to stop.

Twenty years from now if I stay I will forever be looking over my shoulder, waiting, waiting for the next glare, the next sneer, the next mountain of nastiness and I can't do it. I tried again last night to talk to Mum but she was asleep, I checked on Ben and he was asleep too. I feel a smile as I recall brushing his cheek and feeling the warm softness of his skin. That's the last time I will touch him.

I made another mistake. I opened messenger, I shouldn't have. Five messages, one from Dad. What, was he too busy to call and thought a messenger message would do? One from the guy I had been interested in, I got hopeful when I opened that. But it was mean, he ended us before we'd even really started because of what he had 'heard' about me. That cut right through me. And the other three, well, they were from the bitch brigade full of pure hatred. The last line of the last one said 'just kill yourself, you don't deserve life, you're a waste and a joke and we've made you a bigger joke, happy deathday bitch.'

The only part of me that is moving is my hands, they're shaking, I can't breathe. I fumble with my phone, I call Mum, no answer, I call Aunt Helen, no answer, I call Danielle, no answer, I call Tako, no answer. I can't even begin to explain the utter despair and aloneness I am feeling, I really feel like I don't exist, not important enough, not loved enough. I recall Aunt Helen's words but my mind keeps jumbling them up. I call Danielle again, still no answer and that's it, I'm done. I can feel my face wet with tears that I didn't know I was crying.

I can't burden this world any longer, can't waste the earth's air, can't 'be' anymore, it's too much, it's too hard and I'm too weak. I'm a failure and I have failed so I will quit now, leave, depart, end. This is it. Millie, my dog can sense my distress, she's trying to nuzzle me and is pawing at me but I can't respond, I'm too far gone. It's my birthday, it's my birthday and I don't care.

I hear Mum walk past my room, I pray hard that she comes in, finally 'sees' me but she keeps walking past. I hear her go and wake Ben, I hope Ben comes in, he doesn't. I feel invisible and lost, I have tried and done and given so much that I have nothing left. I am nothing left. As though on auto pilot I go to my closet, Millie is watching me and starting to whine quietly. I still ignore her, I adore my dog but I just 'can't'.

I find what I'm looking for and without pause, delay, any thinking, I tie the cord around the closet rail, place the length around my neck and tie it as tight as I can. Then I drop. I feel the fading, I feel it coming, I welcome the nothingness. At the last minute I can feel and hear my pulse struggling, no oxygen, I panic explosively, clawing at the knots, trying to loosen them, trying desperately to untie them but I can't. Everything is buzzing and blurry and I'm getting weaker. I don't want to die, I don't, I want to stop and I'm trying, but I tied the knot too tightly, I dropped too heavily, I need help but help doesn't come.

Millie is whining and clawing at me trying to help me, I wish she could, I wish she had hands, I wish I could break it, tear it, undo it, but I can't. I want to live, I want to live, I want to get well, I want to get help and be well. I can do it, I know I can, I'll be stronger and braver, I swear I'll get help if I can just get myself free but it's too late. I am gone. I have left. I have ended it and I can't come back. I want to come back. Now! I am standing outside myself, I can see my body. Millie is sitting on me looking quizzically at my face, I speak to her, tell her I'm okay and that I'm coming back. She twitches an ear like she sensed something and that's all.

I realise I am gone and the distress hasn't left, I still feel the same, only worse because I can't undo what I have done. Someone is going to find me and be sad and scared, Mum or Ben, I don't want that to happen, I love them too much but it's too late, oh god what have I done. My god, what have I done? I wish with my whole soul that I can be saved. Please, please someone save me. I beg and plead into nothingness, knowing that it's too late, I can't even explain how much regret I feel, it will be a burden I carry into the afterlife.

I want to come back. But it's impossible. Impossible and I regret ending my life. I'm already missing out, missing my morning snuggle with Millie, missing the warm shower water, missing the sunshine, tea and coffee, golden toast with melted butter. I'm going to miss all those little things that make up a day. A smile from a stranger or child, the sound of rain on the roof, the smell of flowers, thunderstorms, ice cream, chocolate, Ben's laugh, Mum's smile, my friends, Aunt Helen. I'm missing out already and I want it back. There is no peace to this and it's final, final. I wish I'd held on and stayed living, stayed alive. Lived.

CHAPTER 10

SPIRIT ANGEL

Oh shit. She did it. I am devastated. Out of frustration I hurl the pot of blue paint I had been using, it splatters against a sheer wall and runs down like blue teardrops down a face.

Out of the corner of my eye I see planet Rosetta Duopolous pulsating with the addition of what was Bree's once vibrant energy. I can't help but cry. I took my eyes off her for a very short time to check on the rest of the globe and I lost her. I feel grief.

I wish I could send her back to her body but it's too late. *Godammit*, it's too late. And I have to say, for the sanity of humanity, please put down those damn devices that take focus off reality, step away from social media, nobody likes a keyboard warrior. Connect in person, nicely and with love. Do all things from a place of love and kindness, even for those who can do nothing for you. Be the goddam change this world so desperately needs to see. Think humans, think! Think about the effect your words have on others, being nasty for no reason is not okay.

CHAPTER 11

AFTER

Millie is barking and scratching at the bedroom door, then running back to the closet and whining and clawing at Bree, then back to the door barking and whining. Bree's spirit is standing in the corner looking shocked at the scene in front of her, seeing herself in the closet, Millie going crazy. The bedroom door is opened from the other side and Mum comes in. She looks around trying to figure out why Millie is so distressed and clearly looking for me as well but not sure where I am. She picks Millie up to soothe her, she walks across my room towards my bed, catching a glimpse of my reflection in a mirror I have on my wall. Instant panic. From her as well as my spirit. Her panic and fear that it's too late. And my panic that she has found me and it *is too late.*

Mum launches herself at me while screaming No, and for Ben to call an ambulance. I watch the scenario unfold before me and it seems to be in slow motion. The ambulance arrives and they come in with a stretcher, my room feels claustrophobic with all the people and activity in it. Mum cradles me in her arms, she is sobbing and saying *no* over and over, it sounds primal, like it is coming from her soul. I so desperately want to be back in my body so I can spare her this pain. Ben is sitting so completely still holding my hand in both of his, he's staring at my face as tears roll down his. I will myself back into my body but it's not working. I can't come back. *It is too late.*

I reach out to touch Mum and Ben but my hands slip through them. I see goose pimples raise on their skin where I have connected, I feel their warmth and long to be back with them. In minutes, my body is wheeled away on a stretcher and my room is still and silent again. Mum and Ben have gone with them. Millie lays on my floor whimpering, I lay and curl my body around her to try and comfort her. I think she senses me, I hope she does because I don't want to leave.

CHAPTER 12

THE FUNERAL

It's my funeral. It's a beautiful sunny day, cloudless sky, warm breeze and I am there, in that coffin, in that chapel, surrounded by my family, my friends, everyone I love. I can't bear to watch but also can't bear to look away, I feel the heavy weight of their sadness and it breaks my heart that I am the reason for it. I didn't know or understand how loved I was, couldn't see it. I sense a 'presence' with me, I know automatically that it's my Grandad. I feel his energy connect to mine and feel him pull me away from the scene in front of me. Next minute we are moving, out of the chapel and into the sunshine.

'Come with me Bree, let's have a wander.'

'But Grandad, I want to watch.'

'Bree, you've seen enough for now'

He takes me instantly to a garden full of flowers that I've never seen before.

'Where are we? I've never seen this before.'

'I made it, it's not real, it's like an illusion. I thought you could do with some colour today. It's a dark day for everyone.'

'I've missed you Grandad.'

'I've missed you too sweetheart.' Bree frowns.

'Grandad, you missed my graduation, you left early, that hurt.' I feel the same sadness I felt when I noticed him missing from the crowd at my graduation. 'Why didn't you stay and watch?'

'Bree, I hid many things when I was alive, like how sick I was and didn't realise. I didn't communicate how I felt. The night of your graduation I was struggling with chest pains but didn't tell anyone as I didn't want to miss seeing you graduate. As you stepped up onto the stage I thought my heart would burst with pride. It made the pain worse. I was dizzy and felt faint so I went outside for fresh air. I had hoped to be able to come back inside in time to see you receive your certificate. I was in quite a state.'

'Oh Grandad, I wish you had told me, I would have understood. So that's why afterwards you left quickly?'

'Yes, I am so sorry Bree.'

'It's okay. I thought I must have upset you somehow.'

'No, you have always been lovely, to me and those around you.'

'And then I didn't get to see you again before you died. I was so confused and upset. I really thought I must have disappointed you somehow.'

'Darling, no, the only time I felt disappointment was when I knew you had left your life, but I had also seen your pain. What you have been through is not okay, what they did to you was not okay, I wish I could come back and kick their asses until eternity but I can't. If I could have come back just to talk to you I would have, I would have stopped you.'

'I couldn't take anymore Grandad, I felt so alone, I felt like such a burden to everyone.'

'Bree, you were a gift, life is a gift. I wish now that I had sought help sooner with my health, but I didn't. I was scared, didn't want to face my fear. So I guess you could say I died of stubbornness by ignoring what was wrong, a common complaint of men I believe.'

I smile for the first time and lean in to Grandad.

'I miss you Grandad.'

'I miss you too blossom. Oh Bree, I sit up here watching life down there and I would sell my soul to the devil to be back amongst life. I am missing so much, watching you and Ben grow, I'm missing out on everyone and everything I used to love to do. I miss the simple things like a lamb roast, beer, golf, I miss the family get-togethers, I miss laughing with you all, I miss being silly with you kids, it's harder on my heart than the pain ever was. I miss your Grandma. I hate seeing how lonely she is now, I miss taking her a cup of tea to her in bed in the mornings, I miss her fluffy morning hair. I miss it all Bree. And this is where my heart hurts for you too. When I got 'here' I saw the futures of my family down there, and they were good. Yeah there was the odd crappy bit like flat car tyres, a garbage bag bursting, the odd life hiccup here and there, but nothing really terrible. Your life Bree, your life was going to get better, the bullying would have stopped, you were headed for happiness, a family, contentment. I wish with all my soul I could have showed you that.'

'Oh Grandad, what have I done?'

He doesn't reply, he just hugs me tightly. I sense a shift in him.

'Come Bree, it's time.'

In what feels like less than a second, he takes me to the graveyard where my burial is beginning. Everyone is gathered around, they are all crying except Ben. I can see he wants to but is trying to be brave for Mum. I watch dumbfounded as they begin to lower my coffin, Grandad has been holding my hand but I break free and rush forward to my family.

'Mum! I'm here!' I stand right in front of her and touch her face. 'Please Mum, please see me here!' She briefly raises her hand and touches her face where I had touched it. I move on to Dad.

'Dad! Dad, I'm here, I'm really here!' I touch his shoulder, he doesn't react. I go to Aunt Helen.

'Aunt Helen! Feel me here, please! I touch her hair, she looks in my direction and straight through me, I think she feels something and then the moment is gone. I move on to Ben.

'Baby bro, I'm here, please Ben, I need you to see me.' I put my arms around him and pull him into a hug, he leans in so slightly and takes a deep breath, he whispers "I miss you Bree." I stay with him, watching as my coffin settles in the bottom of the grave, the final prayer is spoken. I watch as everyone gently tosses a flower into the grave, it feels like slow motion. When it's over everyone quietly starts to move away, Mum and Ben stay at the grave staring sadly into it. I go and stand in between them, holding their hands. Ben looks up at Mum.

'What are we going to do without her Mum?' His eyes search Mum's face.

'I don't know Ben, I don't know.' Mum's face crumples as she embraces Ben, straight through me, for this moment we are bound. It fills my heart to overflowing with love for them and unfathomable sadness that I am here and they are there.

'We just have to keep going Ben, and do the best we can I guess, there is no other way.'

I sense Grandad, he puts his arm around Mum and kisses her cheek, then places his hand on the side of Ben's head. He has tears in his eyes.

'Are you okay Grandad?' he looks at me half smiling, half crying.

'This Bree, this connection, is what I miss the most, the love.'

I nod, I feel it too. Mum pulls back and puts her arm around Ben.

'I guess we should go.'

Ben breaks down crying.

'I don't want to leave her here Mum.'

'Neither do I, not at all.'

'I want her home with us again.' He is sobbing openly.

'Me too Ben, I ache for her, I miss her so much.'

It's killing me all over again to watch them in so much pain and I can't help them or fix it. Grandad takes my hand.

'Bree, I have to go now.'

'Where?'

'Back.'

'Do I go with you?'

'Sadly, for now, no.'

'Where do I go? What happens now?'

'I don't know, someone will come to guide you to where you will be.'

'When will I see you again Grandad?'

'At times I hope we can.'

'I'm scared Grandad.'

'I know baby girl, I know.'

'I want to go home with Mum and Ben.'

'I do too darling, I do too.'

With that, he is gone. Mum and Ben are slowly walking back to Mum's car, they both pause and look back at my grave, where I am, before leaving. I wish I'd held on. And stayed in life.

CHAPTER 13

THE AFTERMATH

Life on earth continues, the gap of where Bree used to be is noticeable. The days seem duller, energy is less. Gloria struggles to face each day, Ben too. Gloria is quick to become teary, the way Ben carries himself seems weighted. Bree's friends still go to message her with the same reflex as in the past, before stopping once they remember she is gone. Aunt Helen paints every day, trying to capture Bree's essence on canvas, she cries openly and freely in her painting studio. Bree's Dad does his best to remain stoic but cries in his car on the way to work. They all long for Bree, wish they could turn back time to when she was there, to hear her voice, her laugh, just have her back with them.

CHAPTER 14

SPIRIT ANGEL

Do you see dear humans? Do you see the ripple effect? Think of when you throw a stone into a still lake, one minute everything is okay and fluffing along nicely and then the next minute you throw a stone and it plops into the water and creates a ripple effect. This is what suicide does to those left behind, this is what negativity does when inflicted onto others. It has an effect. Same goes for positivity too, do or say something nice and it creates an effect. Smile at a stranger. They might be having a crap day and then you smile at them and it makes them feel brighter because you noticed them, you saw them. Sometimes all someone needs is a smile to make them feel better, and you know what else? Smiles are free! So, give them away with abundance!

Another thing that is free is kindness, yes kindness, it costs nothing to be kind. I have no doubt we have all seen a Mum in the supermarket or somewhere, dealing with the challenge of kids and prams or shopping trolleys, looking stressed but holding it together. Next time you see one, don't judge, instead be kind and offer some help. Just like we have all seen elderly people struggle with the hustle and bustle of the modern world. The elderly are often overlooked. Be kind to them, offer them a hand too, they're valid too, listen to them too, they have wisdom to share. Connect. Connect with those around you, in person, Talk, communicate, you never know, you could be saving someone, you could save someone someday. Share your light.

CHAPTER 15

THE RIPPLE EFFECT

DON

I just can't seem to get my shit together anymore. I used to have a stringent routine for life, the same sequence day after day. I'd get up, shower, have breakfast, talk to my family before leaving for work, work all day, go home, have dinner, watch tv or whatever, go to bed then repeat each weekday, always longing for the break of the weekend, not really noticing anything else much. That routine worked for me, it was safe, automatic, but I see now how I had been hiding from life, I don't know why, it was safe, it felt safe. Since losing Bree I find myself lost in grief and regret, grief that my firstborn baby girl has gone, regret that I didn't try harder with her after Gloria and I separated. I thought she was okay, I took it for granted that Gloria would take care of her, she has always been a fantastic mother, I will try harder with Ben now, I owe Bree and Ben that.

Driving to work this morning felt like sensory overload, everything was too loud, too bright, too rushed, just too damn much, I couldn't take it. I pulled over, called my work and told them I was taking a personal day and not coming in, hung up before any questions could be asked. I went to Macca's and brought a coffee, ironically two of Bree's favourite things, then decided to do another of Bree's favourite things and go to the beach.

I didn't care that I must have looked silly being a businessman in slacks, a shirt and tie on the beach with my coffee. Didn't care what anyone thought when I ditched my shoes and socks and rolled up my pant legs to walk barefoot in the sand, I wanted to feel the sand between my toes like Bree loved to do. I see her in my mind's eye doing it, from when she was small, all the way through her life. She would always wriggle her toes down into the warm sand with a small smile on her face, pure joy. There's a lesson there for me, a lesson I will carry in the forefront of my mind for the rest of my life — be in the moment, be present, be aware, find joy in little things. I see now they are the most important. I finally cry, I turn my face to the sky and cry. I manage to pull myself together. Sitting myself on a rock, I hold my coffee cup up to the sky as a toast to the amazing girl Bree was, then I talk out loud to her.

'Hey Bree, it's your Dad, I don't know if you can hear me... What happened to my beautiful girl. I know your mother and I had lots of problems and that's why we separated but I guess I didn't spend enough time with you. I should have talked to you more about it. I can't take it back and I can't get you back. Is this my fault? I feel so guilty that I knew nothing of your pain. I should have paid more attention to you. I miss you so much my darling, I love you Princess.'

I blow a kiss skyward, wishing for one more day with you, even though I know that's not possible. Instead I decide to stay at the beach and spend the day thinking about you and remembering.

AUNT HELEN

In my painting studio alone, I find I am restless, I can't finish projects, I keep going back to the painting I had done for Bree for her birthday, trying to add more light. I feel as though I am somehow trying to replace the light that has gone missing from my world since Bree's death.

I pace the room like a caged animal, finally I give up. I pull out a fresh canvas, pick up a brush, close my eyes and imagine Bree's smiling face. Opening my eyes, I dab the brush on the paint palette, and away I go. It feels good. My hands fly across the canvas as I outline an image of Bree's smiling face, I slow down as I paint her eyes. I finally find the light that had been missing, I add it to her eyes.

'Oh, baby girl, it's your wacky Aunt Helen, coming at you from my studio, just sitting here painting a picture of your beautiful face.' I sigh and slump down onto my stool. 'Why have you done this my darling angel? I miss you so much. You were such a light that flickered ever so brightly, day and night and now your light has been switched off... You've gone and all we have is emptiness, a Bree shaped hole in our hearts. We all miss your bright smile so much.'

I put my hand over my heart and feel tears run freely. With renewed vigour I am determined to finish this canvas, for me, for Gloria, and for Ben. Bree always loved my work, teased me about how I never really took it seriously and that I should sell my paintings, that I and my work was good enough. I used to laugh when she teased me about it but I will listen to her, I will take her words to heart. They are my legacy from her, that I am good enough, that we are all good enough, that we should all believe in ourselves and see that we are good enough. Wise words from my beautiful niece.'

DANIELLE

Wandering through the mall, I see someone out of the corner of my eye that looks like Bree. My automatic response is to call out and wave, but then I remember and I feel lost all over again. Trying to distract myself I go into a shoe shop, I love shoes, I don't need any more but shoes make me happy. I spot a pair of sandals, white with silver glittery sparkles on them, they remind me of Bree so I buy them.

As the salesgirl finalises my purchase the song *How to Save a Life* by The Fray comes on the store music system, an oldie but a goodie. It hits me like a punch. I think back to the missed calls from Bree on the day she left me. I had slept in and was running late, I was in the shower when she called. I tried calling her back on my way to uni but it was too late.

I will always wonder if I could have saved her had I not slept in and were running late. Maybe I could have saved her that day, maybe I couldn't have, I'll never know. I am angry at myself and angry that Bree left me, angry and sad, so horribly sad. I rush out of the shop before I start crying, I make it outside just before my tears of frustration overwhelm me. I fall apart and stomp my way back to my car. Yanking open the car door I throw myself in the driver's seat, crying and talking to Bree.

'You left me! I was, I am your best friend. I am so angry with you! How could you do this to us, all of us? I wanted to grow old with you...! Now what am I going to do?'

I put my forehead on the steering wheel and sob, eventually pulling myself together, driving straight to Macca's drive-thru for a coffee.

TAKO

Trudging home from work in the dark, eating my pizza, every time I hear a noise I look around, hoping to see Bree pull up beside me on her bike. She didn't like me walking home alone at night, either that or she knew I always had pizza. We both loved it but now I always have three slices left over, they were the three she would have eaten.

Carrying the left-over pizza, I see a man walking his dog. He looks down on his luck so I offer him the rest of the pizza, he accepts shyly and I briefly feel good knowing that Bree would have done the same thing. Her kindness knew no bounds. Still walking, I look back and see the man sharing the pizza with his dog and smiling. Even with the weight of missing Bree I smile too, it hits me that I now know how she felt when she shared things. I used to ask her why she was so kind and generous, she shrugged it off and said it was just because it made her feel good to make people happy. She said she couldn't help but share and be kind, she was just wired that way.

I understand it now, like properly know how it feels. She never expected anything back from anyone, and she always said to pay kindness forward. I'm going to make sure I keep doing it, being kind for the simple reason of being kind, no more, no less, just be kind because it's nice and makes everyone feel good. I miss her so much, I feel like an arm has fallen off or something, there's a piece of me missing since she quit life. I look up at the night sky.

'I just want things to be like they were. Danielle and I are your best friends Bree. We had so much fun together, your pain hasn't gone away, it's just been transferred to each and every one of us. I miss you Bree.'

BEN

Coming home from school sucks now, the house is empty, Mum is at work and Bree is dead. Millie is always excited to see me but she doesn't have the same happiness she used to. I guess she misses Bree too but how can a dog tell how it's feeling? Millie has sad eyes most of the time now. I dump my school bag on the floor and go into the kitchen for something to eat, food doesn't taste the same anymore, it's lost its flavour. I decide on a bowl of ice cream with chocolate chip cookies crumbled on it, for a bit extra I add chocolate topping. I stand aimlessly in the kitchen for a minute before deciding to go and eat in my room and stuff around on my computer.

I automatically pause outside Bree's room; the door is open a crack and I wait for a moment. She used to come out to me when she knew I was home and we'd share whatever food I'd made. I'd pretend I didn't want to share and we'd make a game of it and always end up sitting on the couch watching tv talking and eating until Mum got home. I miss it, such a little thing but I miss it so hugely. I can feel myself starting to cry. I push her bedroom door open with my foot and gently sit on her bed, Millie jumps up next to me. I look at where we found Bree, the closet door is closed now. I sit in the silent stillness of her room and close my eyes. I put my hand in my pocket and bring out the locket I'd saved up and got her for her birthday. I carry it everywhere with me.

'Hi sis, It's me. Did I do something wrong? I know we used to fight sometimes but then we would make up and have good, fun times again. It was your 20th birthday and I bought you this locket. I put my photo inside so you would never forget me, wherever you went. You were getting older and seemed to be drifting away from me. I miss our conversations, I miss everything and now I can't talk to you or see you anymore.'

GLORIA

Half of me doesn't want to wake up in the mornings and face another day without Bree, the other half of me says get up, get moving, keep going, Ben needs you. So, I do it, I keep going. Is it getting any easier? No. Is it getting any less painful? No. Bree was my first-born baby. I remember when she was born and I was almost scared to hold her, she seemed so delicate and fragile. I swore I would always love and protect her. I will always, always love her but I feel guilty that I didn't protect her. Mother guilt, but I also didn't know she was still suffering and being bullied. I didn't see that it was still happening and she had been badly scarred, that the hurt continued for her. That's the shit thing about anxiety and depression, you can't see it like you can see a broken leg in plaster or a scar on the surface on the skin. If we could see it that way I am sure we would all have a better understanding. We are all happy to help if we see someone having a hard time with their wheelchair or crutches, we offer a helping hand, so why can't we do the same for people who are struggling with mental illness? Because we can't see it and because the sufferers feel shame at what they feel is weak to admit. I know this now, I wish I knew it then, maybe then Bree would still be here.

I find myself staring into space often, replaying memories in my mind of my family. It comforts me, I miss her so much my heart hurts, losing my child is something I will never get over, never. The only thing I can do is learn to live with the ache, adjust somehow to life without her and do my best for Ben, make sure I always ask if he is okay.

I have slowed down the pace of my life since losing Bree, I had to before I broke down. I have sought help from my doctor, am having counselling, I just still feel so lost without her, Ben does too, I see it in him and it's hard to watch. Nights are the hardest, the silence of the house after Ben is asleep. I find myself checking on him during the nights, making sure he is okay, I watch him sleep sometimes like I did when he was a baby. Once a Mum always a Mum.

I have learnt to be in the moment more too, to not rush all the time, to not always be thinking ahead or worrying about things I can't change. I find it is changing me. I listen more and hear things properly. I wish I had properly heard Bree when she needed me to, that will be a thorn in my side forever, it's my scar. Accepting that she has gone is hard, I want her back, I miss her so incredibly much. I wonder if she's okay wherever she is now, I worry about that. Last thing at night before I try and go to sleep I talk to her, hoping for a sign, praying that she can hear me. Knowing that I can't have her back I wish for a one last time, I pray hard for it.

CHAPTER 16

SPIRIT ANGEL

I have all but abandoned my art project. Taking a leaf out of Ben's book I indulge in the ice cream I was saving for my fireworks, flowers and ice cream creation. Instead I sit and eat the ice cream as I watch the world go by. The ever-present planet Rosetta Duopolous pulsates out of the corner of my eye, it's not improving, it's still more red than green. I wish I could wave a magic wand and make the necessary changes but I can't, it has to be done collectively. The required energy to make it change needs to come from humans connecting and communicating, creating positivity and care between each other, looking out for one another and talking, really talking, not through any devices but face to face, voice to voice. It's important for the continued existence of mankind. Please humans, slow down, connect, embrace, choose life. Choose real life, not screen life, not isolated life, choose connected life. Sure, it may feel a bit awkward to start with, but trust me it's worth it.

I don't know how much time has passed on earth since Bree took her own life, time is a manmade concept, time doesn't exist here. Yeah sure I watch night and day come and go and seasons change from one to another, but those things you humans call clocks, I don't have or need them here. Watching the grief in the aftermath of Bree's passing has been a step, they are talking out loud, it's a start. They will connect to others better now, it's also giving me an idea...

CHAPTER 17

EIGHT MONTHS LATER

GLORIA

Ben and I have been grocery shopping, it's our weekly 'mother and son date'. Plus, Ben complains that I never buy enough snacks so now he comes with me. We have fun, he makes what used to be a tedious chore for me fun. It now costs more but he's happy and that's what I need to see most, so I don't care how much it costs. He's developed an interest in cooking, so we find and try a new recipe every week that we cook together. Not every recipe works but whatever. If we mess it up we go out for pizza instead. It bonds us closer, it keeps our communication open and that is so important. I park outside our house, Ben sees his friend John riding his bike towards us.

'Hey Ben, wanna come over later?

Ben looks at me, I smile and nod.

'Yeah, sure! I'll just help Mum take shopping in.

'Cool! See you soon then!' John waves and rides away.

We take the shopping inside, I start putting it away while Ben walks into the lounge room. He talks to me from the lounge room.

'Do you think she is okay?' Ben asks.

'Who darling?'

'Bree.'

I go into the lounge room, Ben is looking at a framed photo of Bree.

'I think she's okay darling. She isn't struggling or suffering anymore.'

'I really miss her.' I give Ben a hug.

'We all do.' I feel tears starting and I don't want to cry today. Distracting myself I shift my focus on food for ever hungry Ben.

'Now, would you like an orange before you go over to John's?'

'Yes, please.'

'Would you like it skinned or cut into pieces?'

'Cut into pieces. Six pieces and give me two.'

I smile, ruffle his hair then turn to go back to the kitchen for his orange. Ben stays in the lounge room looking at all our family photos.

'Bree never did give me the other piece. It was always four for her and two for me.'

'She probably forgot that you were old enough to eat more.' I call back to him from the kitchen.'

'Yeah, she did that for as long as I can remember.'

I open the cutlery drawer and take out a knife to cut up the orange. Reaching for a plate I bump the oranges in the fruit bowl and one starts to roll along the bench top. I feel a weird, lifting and shimmery feeling come over me.

'Mum!' Ben calls out loudly.

CHAPTER 18

SPIRITUAL UNIVERSE

In a universe far, far away there is a place for the dead that have taken their own lives. This place is called The Flux and it's a space between the spiritual world and the physical world. It's a dark and restless place where the spirits are incredibly sad and scream and yell as if in physical pain, expressing their emotional agony the only way they can. This place, The Flux, stays in suspended animation, where their spirit is trapped until... well, who knows how long. Their spiritual journey is stuck here, they may never be able to fully cross over because it was not their time to die. They changed their universal path by taking their own life.

I, the spirit angel, overseer of the universe, I had an idea earlier about what I can do to try and prevent more suicides occurring. I felt I had to take this chance with Gloria and Bree to hopefully bring about the change in society that so desperately needs to happen. Brace yourselves humans, things are about to get weird...

I have retrieved Gloria from life on earth, I had to. Quite rude of me not to ask her, but a spirit angel has to do what a spirit angel has to do. She has just now arrived into a waiting room.

'Gloria Nachor!' I demand her attention. She looks stunned and scared.

'What's going on? What's happening?'

'Gloria, you will find out in good time.'

'Who are you? What am I doing here?'

I watch her walking around the room, wringing her hands nervously and trying to figure out where my voice is coming from.

'What do you want? What place is this?'

'All in good time.' Gloria is pacing the room.

'One minute I'm in my home talking to Ben, the next minute I'm in this place. This is all too weird.'

Gloria clenches her fists and pummels on the wall.

'Tell me what I'm doing here! Who are you? What's going on? Please... please tell me!' She is close to tears, she cups her hands over her face.

I am watching from a small distance. I turn the room black, startling Gloria again, which I feel bad about but this is what is required to bring about the focus needed. The next step is to bring Bree forward. A golden, semi-transparent wall dividing the room appears, like that of a shimmering waterfall. Bree's spirit gradually appears on the other side of the room. She has a white glow surrounding her. Gloria senses a shift. She turns and sees Bree through the shimmering gold, she screams.

'Mum! It's okay, it's okay.'

'Bree? Is that you?'

'Yes Mum, it is me!'

'Oh my god! Oh, my darling girl, it's you!'

'I've missed you.'

'I've missed you too… We've all missed you. What is this place? Why did you leave us? How can I see you? Gloria starts to cry.

'This place where we are now is not real, but it is a place for us to meet. They want me to talk to you. They want me to show you. I didn't mean to leave, it just happened…'

'How long has it been?'

'I've lost track. There is no time in my world. It's a place of… remember Groundhog Day? Well it's like that except there's no happy ending.'

'It's been eight months, eight hours and about twelve minutes.' Gloria keeps crying.

'Mum, come on, we need to talk.'

'Okay, okay. Talk about what? Do you mean about…?' Bree interrupts her.

'Yes, about what happened. What drove me to this place. About why I'm here and you are there. But firstly, I have to show you something.'

'What?' Bree's spirit walks towards Gloria.

'Hey Mum, do you want to see where I live?'

'If it's all the same to you I'd rather stay here with you.'

'Mum, that won't work. The reason you can see and talk to me now is because of what I have to show you for the future. We need to talk about a lot of things and that will only happen if you come with me.'

'Hmm... so, where is it?'

'I'll take you there.'

'Darling, I'm not so sure about this.'

'You have to see this. I'll bring you back safely, but you really need to see.'

Though hesitant, Gloria wants to seize the opportunity to spend time with Bree so she agrees. I wasn't sure if she would, but it was the chance I knew I would take when I had the idea to bring Gloria here, for her and Bree to talk, really talk.

'Okay, okay!'

Bree reaches through the golden shimmer and grabs Gloria's hand. Gloria receives the same glow that Bree is emitting. The walls that had been surrounding them and the veil that had been separating them all fall away to show a universe full of colours.

'Bree this looks amazing, absolutely beautiful. Is this your home now?'

'Not exactly...'

CHAPTER 19

DARK SPACE

Out of the universe comes a black hole which gets bigger as it heads towards Gloria and Bree. The sound from it is like a huge, roaring ocean wave rumbling to the shore.

'What's going on?' Gloria has to yell to be heard over the noise.

'It's okay Mum. You'll be okay. I've got you. Trust me.' Bree signals to me and I send them down into the black hole. They have a rough journey with a lot of lights, planets, asteroids and stars shooting past them. They are finally spat out when they reach a dark universe. Gloria is hyperventilating as she is having trouble breathing in a universe without air.

'Mum, it's okay. It's okay. You don't need air to breathe here.'

'How do you not need air here?'

'Because this is death Mum. You don't breathe when you're dead.'

'Right you are.' Gloria panics again. 'Am I dead Bree?'

'No, you are just having an experience. Don't think about breathing, just be and you'll be okay.' Gloria calms down into the moment.

'Bree, what have you done?'

'Look at yourself.'

Gloria looks down at herself, she sees that she has the same glow all over her that Bree does.

'What is this? I look just like you!'

'You are like me. It's the only way... I've taken your spirit, soul if you like, and brought you here to show you what I have to deal with now.'

'You've taken my soul?'

'Relax Mum, I'll give it back to you. But you need to see this first hand.'

Bree points to another universe, it is dark with red lightning strikes going off every couple of seconds.

'That's my home. That's where – at this point – that's where I'll spend my eternity.' They stare deeply at each other.

'Oh my...'

Bree puts her finger to her lips.

'Shhh... listen, do you hear that?

Gloria listens intently, she can hear what she thinks is slight screaming.

'What is it?'

Bree turns her head and looks to the direction of The Flux, Gloria looks to the same direction as Bree.

'Here they come.' Bree looks saddened.

CHAPTER 20

THE FLUX

Bree's spirit and Gloria, can do nothing except linger and watch as thousands of spirits rush past them, pausing in their haste and pain only to say a few brief words in their faces.

'I need help.'

'Please help me.'

'Do I matter?'

'It's what I don't say.'

'You could have stopped this.'

'Help me.'

'What's happened to me? Look at me!'

'No! look at me!'

'Do you see?'

'Don't leave me.'

'Do you see the sadness in my eyes?'

A spirit gets up in Gloria's face, yelling at her, startling her.

'Ask me!

She jumps with fear. Gentler this time the spirit speaks again.

'Then ask me again.'

The spirits circle them before drifting back to where they came from.

'Who are they?... And why were they coming at me?' Gloria asks Bree.

'They weren't coming at you. They were talking to their parents... Well, trying to connect with them. There are so many here.'

'So, what is this place?'

Gloria and Bree watch the last of the spirits drift away slowly, one rushes back unexpectedly to try one last time to connect.

'Help me!'

Gloria and Bree look at each other, both shaken up by what they just saw.

'Mum, it's called The Flux. I'm stuck here for now along with thousands of other children and adults. You are in my world now.'

'But what is it?'

'It's situated between the real world... Earth, and the spiritual world. The universe has laws and if you break those laws there is a price to pay. You see Mum, we were not supposed to die. It was not our time. The universe is orderly in its chaos but when you break these laws and the universe becomes unhinged, you end up here. It's all about Universal balance. This place will remain here for eternity. At this point, none of us will ever pass over properly.'

'Oh my god darling, I am so sorry. But how come it's possible that I have contact with you now?'

'We are able to have contact because they want you to do something.'

'But, do what?'

'To let the people know that this is where they end up if they commit suicide... if they take their own lives. You need to take this message back to Earth, back to everyone.'

'This place is horrible and sad,' Gloria exclaims with deep sadness.

'I know Mum, I know...'

CHAPTER 21

ROSETTA DUOPOLOUS

Gloria notices something in the distance behind Bree, a radiant round glow rolling its way towards them.

'Bree, what's that?'

Bree turns and looks in the direction Gloria is pointing.

'Oh that, it's called the Rosetta Duopolous planet.'

'But what is it? I've never seen anything like it.'

'It holds all the thoughts, actions and words from the beginning of time. Everything that has taken place or has been thought or said, both positive and negative, is held in this planet. Actually, it's more like the size of a solar system.'

'Do the colours have any significance?'

'Yes, Red is negative, everything negative, and green is positive, everything positive.'

'There seems to be a lot more red than green.'

'You're right. I want you to see this.'

Bree raises her hands and closes her eyes for a moment, then a video collage appears from the planet featuring Bree, a visual display of Bree's emotions before she committed suicide. Gloria watches it with tears in her eyes.

'Love, hate, miss you, kind, despair, lost, I can't, now, beaten, trust, finished, hurt, anger, friends, smile, cry, pain, loss, laughter... not.'

At the end of the collage Bree blows a kiss and forms a heart shape with her fingers. Then more letters appear, forming words that glow in front of them.

'Die you bitch!'

'You're fat and SOOO ugly!'

'Let's hear it again how you slit your wrists?'

'Why did it take so long for you to kill yourself?'

Gloria watches horrified and stunned.

'Oh, this is horrible. Why didn't I know about this?'

Bree shrugs and disregards Gloria's question.

'If it stays red for a period of time without changing back to green then your world will implode.'

'Implode?'

'Yes, the surface of the earth will collapse in on itself and slide into the centre, just like a giant sink hole. Then the earth will explode, destroying mankind forever. There is too much negativity in your world. It's been a slow but steady decline into constant negativity in every way, from selfishness, greed, meanness, nobody can see past themselves anymore, nobody is even taking care of nature anymore, it all adds up.'

'Oh my god! What can be done?'

'The adults have to take charge. That's what they should be doing anyway. The adults and children of this generation have to change the direction of the world, and the only way to do that

111

is for the adults to step up and change the way they mentor their children, change what they show and teach their children.'

'How did you become so knowledgeable?'

'The Spirit Angel showed me the end of the world. It isn't that far away and that is why you are here now.'

Rosetta Duopolous comes closer, Bree and Gloria notice, neither understanding why. A new video emerges from it, the visual surprises Bree.

'Oh wow, I haven't seen this before...'

Video is shown from the aftermath of Bree's funeral, showing her the pain of her family and friends since then. Bree starts to cry as she watches. Then she is shown a video of current life time, of what her friends are doing now without her. Bree becomes hysterical, shaking and crying, she throws her arms around Gloria who savours the embrace.

'Oh god Mum, what have I done?'

Bree clings on to Gloria and in that moment, they are spun away into the universe. The Rosetta Duopolous planet continues on its path.

CHAPTER 22

THE BLACK ROOM

The universe disappears as Gloria and Bree are delivered into the black room. Gloria, unused to such extreme energy shifts, has fainted on the floor upon arrival into the black room. She comes to and slowly starts to get up. Bree watches and waits.

'Oh, Bree! Are we back?'

'Yes. Look I know we should have talked about a lot of things but we didn't, for whatever reason. But we need to. I need to.'

'Okay. Why did this happen?'

'No Mum, it's not about why did this happen. It's about why did I do it?'

'But it's the same thing, isn't it?' Bree starts

pacing the room.

'It's not the same thing, it's far from the same thing. Saying why did this happen makes it sound like I had some sort of accident. Why did I do it

114

means I must have made a conscious choice... but I didn't.'

'Darling, calm down.'

Being told to calm down makes Bree angry.

(Sidenote – Spirit Angel here, sorry, I couldn't help but stick my nose in and say that never in the history of me overseeing the world has anyone that's ever been told to calm down, actually calmed down. Just sayin').

'I'm not going to calm down! You're my mother! You were supposed to protect me! Dad too! And neither of you did! I'm pissed off that neither of you were there!'

Gloria moves toward Bree.

'That's not fair Bree. I was there! I was always there for you!'

'I'm pissed off that everyone closed their eyes after my death and did nothing! It's like I just disappeared... that I didn't exist! You all kept everything inside and did nothing! I'm super fucking annoyed that all these deaths are preventable yet no one does anything. No-one gives a shit. They would rather call suicides accidental deaths as a way to brush the reality aside... Like I accidentally hanged myself.'

'Oh darling, I thought you were okay, I honestly did. I wish you had told me that you were still having problems with those bullies.' Bree looks downcast.

'I know, I should have, everyone's lives were so busy and I felt like a burden.'

'Bree, you never once were a burden in any way. But why on your 20th birthday?' Bree starts to cry.

'I'm not sure. As you can understand, if I was thinking logically I wouldn't have done this... Oh god Mum, what have I done to everyone?' To you, to Ben, to Dad and my beautiful friends who I will never see again... What have I done?'

Bree breaks down, Gloria can only hold her while she cries.

'Oh, my sweetheart.'

Bree pulls herself together and faces Gloria.

'So, has anything changed?'

'With what?'

'Has my death been a waste? Have they changed the laws? What are they doing to help the victims of bullying?'

Gloria stumbles over her words for a moment.

'Some schools have hired trained counsellors to manage the effects of bullying on the students.'

Bree slowly closes her eyes in emotion and frustration.

'Tell everyone Mum! You have to take this message back! It's not about managing the effects of bullying. If you get rid of the cause then there are no effects to deal with. There needs to be some sort of punishment for these bullies. The laws need to be changed!'

CHAPTER 23

SPIRIT ANGEL

I think it's time I intervened. Bree is emotional and distressed, and Gloria is concerned for Bree and fearful of being capable of bringing about the changes that need to happen. I make my way into the room, I gently light it up so as not to startle them. They both sense my presence and turn to face me.

'Hello ladies.' I curtsy for fun then get straight to the point. 'So, Gloria, your world is in trouble. Why is it so? All these people are dying around you, some you know, others you don't, but believe me it's happening and it's happening way too much.' Gloria looks stunned but I know I have her full attention. I pause knowing she wants to speak.

'Who... who, what are you?'

'Who am I? Here they call me the Spirit Angel, however I prefer to be known as pure positive energy. I am what humans refer to as their choice of God title, whichever religion they choose to follow, whatever, it doesn't matter. We are all the same. Please allow me to apologise for briefly taking you from your earth life to come here and bringing you on a journey of discovery and pain. It was never my intention to cause distress. But, as Bree has told you, this is where your world is heading unless you do something.'

I start pacing the room, I can't help it, it is difficult for me to not be able to save the ones who choose to leave. I used to be able to, but now there are so many every day that I can't keep up.

'Don't you get it? You need to talk about it, to the government, the schools, everyone on your planet needs to talk about it. You talk about depression and getting help, but never talk about the final resting place, of those that commit suicide. It is swept away like it doesn't exist, and all the time your people, in your world, are taking their own lives! Committing suicide! Wake up! It has become an epidemic! A distressing and unnecessary epidemic and you need to fix this problem. Your planet needs a united front and new laws. One life wasted is one too many.' Gloria has listened intently this whole time, I am very relieved to know that. I dare to believe that change will come, it needs to.

'But how? Where do I start? How do I start? I'm just a Mum, a working Mum, I don't know where to start.'

'You start with a conversation, to a principal, a politician, you start making yourself heard, it will gather momentum. Gloria, I beg of you, please do this. I could show you thousands of situations unfolding all across the globe right this minute, of people either thinking of ending their lives or actually doing it. I can't do anything anymore aside from greet them when they arrive and send them onto the next part of their journey. What day is it today on Earth?'

'It's still Sunday... I think!' Gloria looks confused, poor woman. I think I've put her into quite a muddle but I know she is capable. She has the grace and wisdom to be heard and start making the changes.

'These preventable deaths will happen again tomorrow, and the next day, and the day after that, so many beautiful and prosperous lives disappearing from Earth. It's tragic, it has to stop.'

I think for now, my work with Gloria is done, I start to recede from them.

'Oh, one more thing, why is it always God's will when you humans do something that is destructive to mankind, yet when you do something good for humanity it's always your will? Just a thought, perhaps ponder that.'

I start to drift from them.

'You need to talk. You need to love and take care of each other!'

I send them back to the room with the gold, shimmery waterfall-like walls. Bree walks towards the centre of the room.

'Mum, I have to go now. I love you all.'

Gloria walks towards Bree, she gives her one last hug.

'My darling, can't you stay a little while longer?'

'No, I only had this small window of opportunity.' The shimmery wall is between them now, they hadn't noticed it drift towards them.

'Oh darling, I love you so much! Will I see you again?'

Bree is starting to recede and fade away.

'No Mum, but I am always around you.' Bree blows a kiss to Gloria, smiles a small smile, then fades away. The room starts to turn black, with Gloria standing in a beam of light. She is unaware, her eyes searching for where Bree went. She faintly hears Bree's voice in the distance.

'Remember, the laws need to be changed to protect the innocent children. I know you can do this Mum, I love you.'

CHAPTER 24

HOME ON EARTH

'Mum!'

Ben snaps Gloria back into the present moment, tears rolling down her face. The orange is still rolling across the bench, she catches it as it falls. Ben walks into the kitchen, Gloria quickly rubs away the tears.

'Yes darling?'

'I'm grown up now so I want the extra slice.' He

looks intently at Gloria.

'Have you been crying?'

Gloria cuts the orange into six pieces and lays them onto two plates. Three pieces and two pieces. She leaves one slice sitting on the benchtop.

'Um... yes well...'

Ben interrupts her.

'It's not a women's problem thing, is it?'

'No… Um…' Gloria feels flustered all of a sudden.

'Because you had one of those last week.'

Gloria hands the plate to Ben and starts to leave the kitchen.

'Ben, it's not a women's problem thing.' Women don't call it a problem.'

Ben takes the plate and starts to wander out of the kitchen.

'So this is what my life has become…'

He pauses as he leaves the room, adding some drama to his movement and expression.

'God it's a lot to deal with for a twelve-yearold.'

Gloria smirks at him, her eyes glistening. She picks up her plate with the two slices and follows him out of the kitchen.

'Hey Ben, I need to tell you a story, a strange but true one. Then we have got a lot of work to do,

I'll need your help.'

The single slice of orange on the bench is rocking gently by itself.

'Okay cool. What's the story about?' Gloria

takes a deep breath in.

'Bree, her life. Then we have a lot of work to do. For Bree, and for the greater good of all of us.'

The slice of orange disappears from the bench in a gold shimmery mist.

In the lounge room, Gloria sinks down into an arm chair. Ben had slung himself onto the couch. He flicks through tv stations, stopping on a music channel. Gloria tells Ben about her experience with Bree. Ben is shocked but listens intently. He is trying to be brave and not cry but can't help it.

Gloria gets up, opens a cupboard and takes out a family photo album. She goes and sits next to Ben, hugs him briefly and opens the album, they are soon laughing together at some of the photos. Ben looks at Gloria as she closes the album. He sees the conflict of sadness for Bree and happiness for him in her eyes. He feels like he has suddenly grown up.

'Mum, we can do this, I will help, we need to make things right, for Bree and for everyone else that needs it. We can do it, I know we can. So, let's do it.'

Gloria looks at Ben, her heart bursting with pride.

'Yes, let's do it.'

Ben grins at her.

'Seal it with a high five then Mum!' Gloria cracks up laughing but high fives Ben anyway.

'Alright! Go Mum!'

Still smiling, Gloria picks up their plates and heads to the kitchen. She notices a music video on the tv screen and stops to watch it.

'Wow, this is a beautiful song. Do you know what it's called Ben?'

'*Hold on*, that's what it's called, it's cool hey.'

'It really is.'

Ben turns the volume up slightly. He feels a shiver go through his body, he swears he hears Bree singing.

'I am praying that this song reaches you.'

Ben raises his eyebrows and puckers his lips, then leaps off the couch to follow where Gloria went.

'Mum, something weird just happened. I swear I heard Bree singing along to that song.'

'I don't think that's weird darling, I think that's cool, she did tell me she is always around us.'

CHAPTER 25

SPIRIT ANGEL

THOUGHTS

My dear humans, life is good, then sometimes it has crappy times, and then it becomes good again. Nobody has it all together, myself included, but hang in there for the good and when it's crap then think of the good. Night time, nights are usually when our thoughts magnify and unravel. Nights can be hard and lonely. I ask you to think of this in the dark times and to reach out to someone if you're feeling low.

Connect, communicate and know that a new day is coming, the sun will come up again. Be in the moment. Whatever you're doing, be present, slow down. Go outside and walk barefoot on grass, wriggle your toes in sand, feel the wind on your face and sun on your skin, taste food, try new things, laugh, laugh a lot, listen to others and hear them.

You are all important, you are all valuable, even on the bad days. Feel love, give love, smile, give smiles away, you never know, a smile can save a soul. Be kind, to yourself and to others, always be kind. Find your passion and live it, live a curious life. Be yourself, be comfortable in your skin. Choose to feel happy and if it's a bad day then choose to be okay and get through the day knowing there's a fresh one tomorrow. Put down the devices, look up, breathe fresh air, drink plenty of water, but most of all choose life, please always choose life.